Gliding

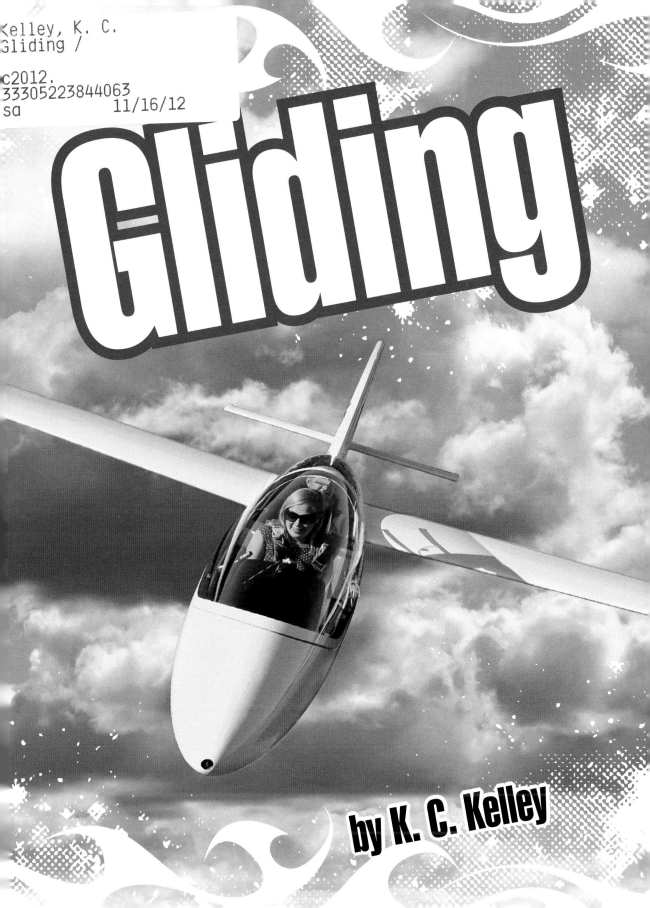

by K. C. Kelley

Published by The Child's World®
1980 Lookout Drive
Mankato, MN 56003-1705
800-599-READ
www.childsworld.com

The Child's World®: Mary Berendes, Publishing Director
Shoreline Publishing Group, LLC: James Buckley Jr.,
    Production Director
The Design Lab: Design and production

ISBN 9781609732073
LCCN 2011940082

Photo credits: Cover: iStock.
Interior: Corbis: 7, 8, 24; dreamstime.com: Mikael
Damkier 4, Aleksander Lorenz 11, Matus Mihalcin 16,
Nelson Hale 19 (background); iStock: 28; Photos.com:
12, 15, 20, 23; Titian Scholtmeyer/SSA: 19 (diagram);
Wikimedia: 27.

Printed in the United States of America

Table of Contents

Swooping high above the earth, a glider rides the winds.

CHAPTER ONE

Free as a Bird!

Jet aircraft need a huge, powerful engine to take to the sky. Small private planes need motors and rapidly spinning propellers to fly. Balloonists might float without an engine, but they can't really steer. And skydivers head to earth as soon as gravity grabs them.

People use all these ways to reach the sky. Still, people cannot truly fly like birds unless they have engines, props, parachutes, or other things.

However, there is one type of flyer who can: the glider pilot.

Soaring above the earth without engine or motor, swooping from place to place with enormous wings, flying a glider is as close to being a bird as humans can get. Glider pilots talk about the freedom they feel when they're **aloft**. There's no rattling and shaking of many parts. They have the perfect experience of simple flight.

Gliders are long-winged aircraft that fly without the use of motors. They were among the first types of aircraft made by people. The famous Italian inventor Leonardo da Vinci designed glider wings in the 1500s. Many other daring people have leaped off heights with homemade wings, though not all of them landed safely.

In the 1800s, a pair of Europeans made the first successful gliders. Starting in 1891, Otto Lilienthal of Germany made more than 100 safe flights beneath his wide wings. Others made improvements, including Octave Chanute and John Montgomery.

In the early 1900s, two American brothers, Orville and Wilbur Wright, added an engine to their glider wings. Of course, that became the first airplane. The Wright Brothers often gave credit to earlier flyers for their **inspiration**.

Early gliders fought the forces of gravity.

Famous pilot Charles Lindbergh flew this early glider in 1930.

Airplanes with motors and engines **dominated** flight. But the idea of flying without power remained a goal. Many pilots wanted to have a less-noisy, more-birdlike flight. In 1911, in fact, Orville Wright set a world record for glider flight of nine minutes.

As more and more inventors looked at gliding, or soaring, as it is also known, one problem stood out. They could get the gliders to take off from a height and simply glide until gravity brought them down. But they were having trouble actually steering the gliders. That is, they could not yet really fly them . . . just ride them.

A discovery in the 1920s changed all that. Pilots found that they could catch currents of rising air from the ground to make their gliders rise. This is called "lift," and is the key to sports such as soaring, hang gliding, and parasailing.

With this discovery, newer and better wings were created to let gliders fly in rising air. By the 1950s, there were enough glider pilots to hold world championships. The sport grew rapidly. Many pilots formed glider clubs to learn from each other. They learned to launch the gliders towed by powered aircraft, which let them reach new heights.

The 1980s and 1990s saw many changes that made gliding even better. Most of these were instruments that helped the pilots find the best air. Other inventors used space-age materials to make the gliders stronger and lighter. As gliders continue to be improved, for pilots who love to fly . . . the sky's the limit.

Today's gliders are perfect for flying above beautiful landscapes.

Running the Show
The Soaring Society of America (SSA) was formed in 1932 to organize the growing sport. Today, they work with clubs around the country to make sure gliding is safe. They also help select Americans to take part in international events. The SSA also provides information to people who would like to take up gliding.

The pilot sits in the cockpit before takeoff. The canopy will drop down to cover him.

CHAPTER TWO

Gliding Basics

A modern glider looks a lot like an airplane, but with some important differences. (In fact, gliders can also be called "sailplanes.") Like airplanes, gliders have wings attached to a long, thin body. Glider wings, however, are much longer. They are also more narrow. Glider wings also have some moving parts as on an airplane.

While airplanes have several wheels for landing, a glider has one. It is located under the pilot's **cockpit**. Inside the glider, the pilot uses a control stick to steer. He uses foot pedals to turn and on land. An instrument panel shows the pilot how high he is, and how fast he's going, among other things. A **GPS** lets him know exactly where he is on the earth. A radio connects him to people on the ground. A clear plastic **canopy** covers the pilot and gives him a view all around. Most gliders can only hold one person at a time.

The first gliders were made of wood covered by canvas. Today, most gliders are made from very strong and light types of plastic. Their outsides are very smooth to help them slide easily through the air. The nose of a glider is also very pointed for the same reason.

Panels on the long, thin wings move up and down to steer the glider. On the tail of the glider, other controls help the glider move up and down.

Gliders come in many sizes, but most have wings from 40-90 feet (12-28 m) wide. They don't weigh very much—about 500-1,500 pounds (227 kg-680 kg). They can be taken apart and towed behind a car. This makes it easy for glider pilots to visit different places in search of new places to soar.

A new glider might cost about $30,000–50,000, but some pilots can find used ones for about $10,000. Gliders used in competition by top pilots can be worth nearly one million dollars.

Here's a good look at the long, narrow wings of a glider.

The small plane (right) tows the glider
into the air with a long rope.

Learning to be a glider pilot can take many hours. Pilots must have a **license** from the U.S. government to fly. This is so that both pilots and other aircraft can be safe in the sky. Glider pilots fly with teachers in special two-person gliders. The instructor shows the student how the controls work and makes sure the student learns the right way. Student pilots also study in books and must take tests to prove their knowledge.

To finally earn their license, pilots must complete a solo flight. After checking wind conditions, the pilot climbs into the glider. It is attached to a small airplane by a long, strong rope. As the airplane rolls down the runway, the glider is towed along, balancing on its one wheel. Once in the air, it is pulled behind, much as you might see a flying banner pulled behind a plane.

When they are high enough, the glider pilot releases the rope. The small plane returns to the ground. Alone, the glider pilot soars into the sky in silence.

Remember lift? Understanding lift is the most important part of gliding. The pilot must study the ground below him and the clouds around him to find it. There are three basic types of lift:

- **Thermals** are areas where the warm ground below heats the air above. All warm air rises, creating areas of lift that are perfect for gliding. Pilots watch for clouds that form in these areas. They also might see birds doing the same thing: floating on warm air. A glider pilot can often circle around and around in a thermal **column**.

- Ridge lift is found when wind hits a hill or mountain. As it hits the higher land, moving air "bounces" upward. This upward bounce can lift the glider up very nicely.

- Wave lift is also found around hills and mountains. In this type of lift, the wind has blown over the top of the higher ground. It goes up on the far side.

By finding lift, the glider pilot can stay aloft for a long time, eye to eye with the birds.

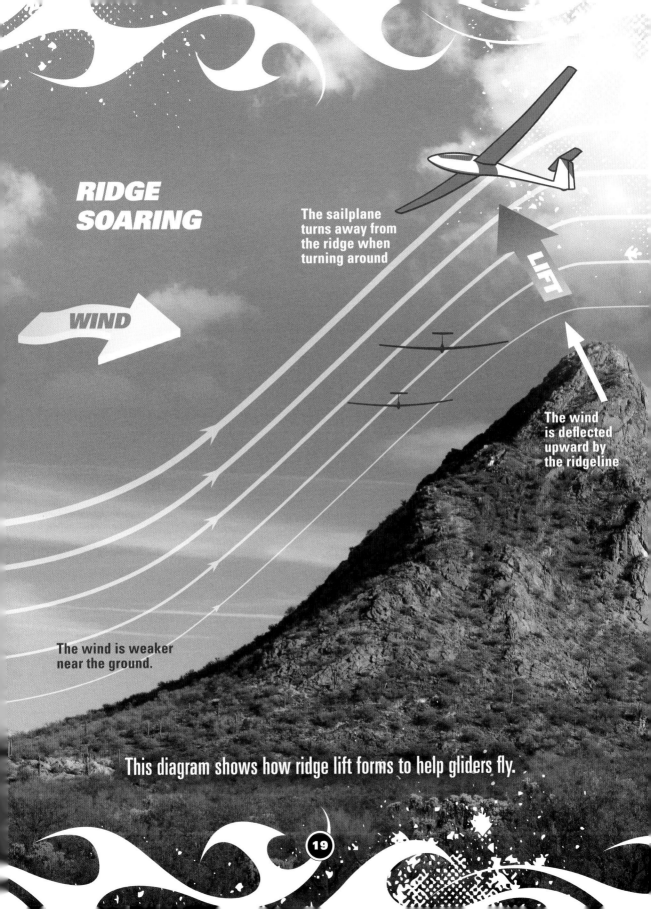

RIDGE SOARING

WIND

The sailplane turns away from the ridge when turning around

LIFT

The wind is deflected upward by the ridgeline

The wind is weaker near the ground.

This diagram shows how ridge lift forms to help gliders fly.

Nature's Gliders

Two animals use gliding skills similar to those used by human pilots. Both flying squirrels and sugar gliders, who live in Australia, have skin flaps between their limbs. They can expand the flaps as wings to help them glide through the air from tree to tree.

Coming in for a landing: Notice the single wheel.

Glider rides can last for an hour or 10 hours . . . or more, depending on the weather. A pilot who can find more and more thermals can stay out longer. Eventually, however, all glider rides end.

When it's time to land, the pilot slowly steers the glider toward the landing zone. He tries to come in at a very low angle, guiding the plane straight toward the landing. He gets closer and closer to the spot and just as he's over it, he puts the wing flaps down. This slows the aircraft. It also removes the lift that keeps the glider aloft. Slower and much lower, the glider then lands smoothly on its one wheel. The wing tips remain off the ground as the glider slowly rolls to a stop, helped by flaps that pop up on the wings.

When the glider finally stops, one wing tips gently to the ground. Then the pilot can pop the canopy and climb out. And if the weather's good . . . there might be time for one more flight before sunset!

CHAPTER THREE

Stories from the Sky

Glider pilots soar above the earth for the love of flight. Most fly simply for the chance to experience life as a bird. Others use gliding for different reasons.

The most famous examples of gliders in history came during World War II. In the 1944 D-Day assault, British and American glider pilots delivered hundreds of soldiers behind enemy lines. The gliders swooped in at night without being heard by people below. These soldiers could then carry out important secret missions.

These gliders were much larger and could carry dozens of soldiers. Also, they were just used once. After landing, they could not be re-launched.

Other large gliders helped deliver heavy gear such as tanks or trucks. By the 1950s, helicopters were doing the military work that gliders had done.

This photo from a museum shows the cockpit of a World War II glider.

Aerobatic glider pilots can do loops!

Other glider pilots take to the sky to win medals. International and national meets are held. Pilots compete for distance and speed. They have to steer their gliders through courses of different lengths.

In 2010, the Open Class champion was Michael Sommer of Germany. He also won in 2006 and 2008. Many European pilots are among the best in the world.

In 2009, the most recent women's world event, the champion was Nathalie Hurlin of France. Women don't fly gliders nearly as much as men do, but they can look to Nathalie for inspiration.

The last American winner at the world championships was George Moffat in 1974.

Another type of soaring is **aerobatics**. This sport involves performing daring moves such as spins and tight turns while gliding. In 2009, three pilots from France won the team competition. Georgij Kaminski of Russia was the overall champion.

Soaring groups also keep world records. Klaus Ohlmann of Germany currently holds several records. Over his long soaring career, he has set more than 30!

In January 2011, he flew a record 1,087 miles (1,750.6 km) over a triangular course. On the same day, he set a speed record of 76.2 miles per hour (122.75 kph). Both set new world marks.

The women's distance record over a three-side course was set by Susanne Schodele in 2010. She covered 653 miles (1,051.4 km).

Other records cover cross-country flying, or free distance. They measure how far a glider can go in a roughly straight line over a wide area of land. The longest flight for many years was by Thomas Knauff, who covered 1,023 miles (1,646 km) in one flight in 1983. However, Ohlmann topped that mark several times. His longest flight was in 2010. He soared across Argentina for a distance of 1,395 miles (2,245.6 km).

Klaus Ohlmann has piloted this glider to many world records.

Gliders in Space?

The idea of flying without a motor was used in the space shuttles. As the shuttles come in for a landing, they are simply enormous gliders. They soar down toward earth without any motor or engine power. The pilot steers the plane in a long, low flight just as a glider pilot does to a safe, smooth landing.

Klaus Ohlmann

SEIKO

University of Stuttgart
Germany

Gliding is a challenging sport, but it can really give you wings!

The highest glider flight was 49,009 feet (14,899 m) by Robert Harris in 1986 in California.

Pilots of gliders travel the globe to find the best places to fly. Remember, they need lift, and you can't always find that in your backyard.

California's Sierra Nevada mountains provide some great lift. The ridges of the Appalachians in Pennsylvania draw many gliders to that state. In southern Texas, the hot weather creates perfect thermal conditions.

In Europe, the Alps in France and Switzerland are often the site of championship flights. Germany is also home to many mountain spots that are great for gliding. South Africa, too, boasts numerous gliding hot spots.

Wherever they go, glider pilots love their sport.

"There is a great joy in soaring quietly above a beautiful terrain," says glider pilot Russell Crane. "I love the challenge of staying aloft using just my skill to find the lift that nature provides."

Glossary

aerobatics—acrobatic moves performed by aircraft

aloft—up in the air

canopy—a covering, in the case of gliders, over the pilot's seat

cockpit—the pilot's seating area

column—a tall cylinder

dominated—took control of

GPS—Global Positioning System, it uses satellites to track locations of things on Earth

inspiration—something or someone who helps give a person strength or ideas to improve or grow

license—a document that gives a person official permission

thermals—columns or waves of warm air rising from the ground

Find Out More

BOOKS

Sugar Gliders
By Elizabeth O'Sullivan (Lerner Books, 2008)
Take a closer look at nature's most famous gliders.

The World Record Paper Airplane Book
By Jeff Lemmers (Workman, 2006)
Use the patterns in this book, and your imagination, to build your own paper gliders and airplanes.

The Wright Brothers' Glider
By Gerry Bailey and Karen Foster (Crabtree, 2008)
This illustrated story shows how experiments by the Wright Brothers with gliders led to the creation of airplanes.

WEB SITES

For links to learn more about extreme sports: **childsworld.com/links**

Note to Parents, Teachers, and Librarians: We routinely verify our Web links to make sure they are safe and active sites. So encourage your readers to check them out!

Index

About the Author

K.C. Kelley enjoys writing books for young readers. He has written about baseball, football, and soccer, as well as about animals, astronauts, and other cool stuff. His friend Russell Crane, an expert glider pilot, was a huge help in preparing this book.